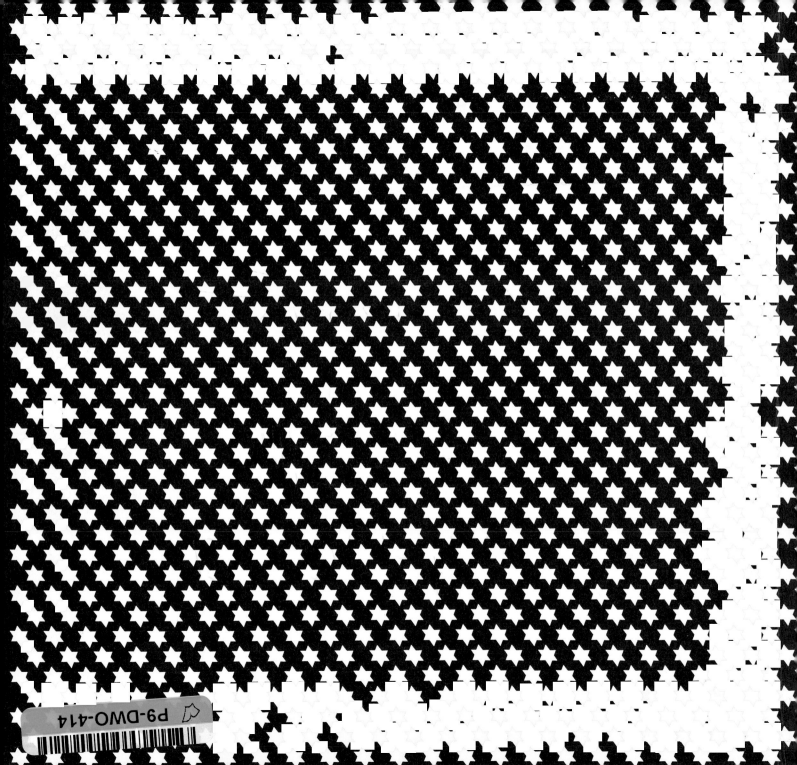

To Matthew,

All my best

Sheldon Oberman

TV SAL AND THE GAME SHOW FROM OUTER SPACE

Story by Sheldon Oberman

Illustrations by Craig Terlson

★★★★★★★★★
NORTHERN LIGHTS BOOKS FOR CHILDREN

Red Deer College Press

Northern Lights Books for Children are published by
 Red Deer College Press
 56 Avenue & 32 Street Box 5005
 Red Deer Alberta Canada T4N 5H5

Acknowledgements
Edited for the Press by Tim Wynne-Jones.
Design by Avril Orloff.
Printed and bound in Canada by D.W. Friesen Ltd. for Red Deer College Press.
Financial support provided by the Alberta Foundation for the Arts, a beneficiary of the Lottery Fund of the Government of Alberta, and by the Canada Council, the Department of Communications and Red Deer College.

The Alberta
Foundation
for the Arts

Providing a foundation for the arts

THE SOURCE
OF MANY BENEFITS

Canadian Cataloguing in Publication Data
 Oberman, Sheldon.
 TV Sal and the game show from outer space
 (Northern lights books for children)

ISBN 0-88995-093-8

I. Terlson, Craig.   II. Title.   III. Series.
PS8579.B47T2   1993   jC813'.54   C92-091843-3
PZ7.0247Tv   1993

To my daughter, Mira Oberman,
who inspired this story. — *S.O.*

For my own TV Sals:
Eli, Reba, and Tess. — *C.T.*

TV Sal was watching TV at the cottage.
She had been watching all week long.

Her father said, "That TV will suck your brain as empty as an old grapefruit."

Her brother said, "Your eyes will be as square as that TV screen."

Her mother asked, "Would you like to do something different, dear? Come out with us to look at the fog."

"No, thanks," said Sal. "I want to watch the *Pretty Piggy Supersweet Special*. Then the *Top Fifty Video Thriller Countdown*. After that, there's a cartoon show about monster garbage cans."

"Call us if you want us," they said. "We won't go far."

But something was wrong with Channel Two.

There was no *Pretty Piggy Supersweet Special.*

There was a game show that Sal had never seen before.

She decided to change the channel.

"DON'T TOUCH THAT DIAL! ♪♪

yelled the game show host. "I'm Jack Dee Doobie, and you could be . . .

OUR ★NEXT★ BIG ★ WINNER! ♪♪

"How?" asked Sal.

"Bring me everything on this list," he said. "Then . . .

☆ LET'S MAKE A TRADE! ☆

Sal read the list:

- a litre of rocket fuel
- eight expanding pressure straps
- three quartz ball bearings

Sal didn't know what they were.
So she found what she could
around the cottage:

☑ a bottle of diet cola,
  ☑ eight rubber bands
    ☑ and some glass marbles.

"Come on in!" yelled Jack Dee Doobie.

...BUZZAT!

Sal was buzzatted right inside the television.

"Give me those parts," said Jack Dee Doobie. "And I'll trade you . . .

A CHANCE TO WIN!"

"Win what?" asked Sal.

"A BIG PRIZE!" said Jack Dee Doobie. "Just spin the wheel. You have to land on fifty-seven. Then you can try our backward spelling contest. If you win, you tell your most embarrassing secret.

If we laugh loudly enough, you pick the weirdest person in the audience for a date. If the judges like your choice, you can trade your date for a Big Prize. Now, isn't that easy?" asked Jack Dee Doobie, all smiles.

"No, it's not easy," said Sal. "And what is the Big Prize?"

"A meteorite scale!" said Jack Dee Doobie.

"OOH!" went the audience.

"Or an air tank in one of four shades of grey!"

"AAH!" went the audience.

"Or last but not least . . . "

"Forget it," said Sal.
"No trade."

"Please!" he begged.
"We need those parts to fix our
spaceship!"

"AHA! You tried to trick me,"
said Sal. "You're aliens from
Outer Space!"

"It's true!" said Jack Dee
Doobie.

"But we crashed and we can't get home. I'll trade you my Universal Channel Changer! It puts you on any TV show in the universe."

Sal's eyes lit up. She said,

"YOU'VE GOT A TRADE!"

The audience went wild.

Sal pressed Channel Five.

BRUM ☆ GRUZZEL

She was on another TV show.
But not one from this world.

BEEP ★ HAZAP

It was *The Planet Goofalot Cooking Show*.
And Sal was the main dish. The chef lifted her
by the ankles and stuck her in a pot.

Quickly, she switched back to Channel Two.
Only to hear Jack Dee Doobie say. . .

"Our show is over for today, folks.
See you tomorrow on

LET'S ★ MAKE ☆ A ☆ TRADE! "

"Wait!" cried Sal. Too late.
Another show was starting.

"It's *GORBEE NIGHT LIVE!*" an announcer said. "The greatest talent show in Outer Space.

Our next act is Al from the Planet Dirt—I mean Sal from the Planet Earth!—foreign names always mix me up!"

Sal didn't know what to do.

She grabbed what looked like four rocks
and began to juggle.

"*RAU–AWK!*" the rocks screamed.

"You're juggling THE ROCKONS!"
the announcer yelled. "They're the
greatest rock band in the galaxy!"

Sal dropped them on the floor.

"I'm sorry," she said. "Oh, I wish
I'd never met Jack Dee Doobie.
If he hadn't crashed his space ship,
I wouldn't even be here."

"*RAU–AWK!*" yelled THE ROCKONS, hopping toward Sal. "*RAU–AWK* Sal!"

Quickly, Sal pressed the Universal Channel Changer.

BRUM ★ GRUZZELBEEP ★ HAZAP ★

She got away . . .

And found herself on *The Planet Barkaloon Comedy Show.*

Barkaloons think only one thing is funny—slopping each other with paint and slopping Sal, over and over again.

Just as Sal got her turn to slop paint back, THE ROCKONS showed up shouting, "*RAU–AWK* Sal!"

Sal only just escaped . . .

BRUM ★ GRUZZELBEEP ★ HAZAP!

To Channel Ninety-Nine . . .

"Welcome to *THE MEEBLY MAWBLY MIDNIGHT MONSTER MOVIE*," the announcer said. "Our movie tonight is called

THE HORRIBLE ONE-HEADED, TWO-EYED, TEN-FINGERED CREATURE FROM ACROSS THE UNIVERSE."

That horrible creature was Sal.

She switched to Channel One Hundred and One — *The Planet Groan Exercise Show.*

Channel One Thousand and Fifty — *The Mud and Crud Beauty Contest.*

Channel Forty-Four Thousand — a talk show on
Planet Finkelouie where the host had five heads.

"Will one of your heads please tell me how to get
home?" Sal begged.

But the heads wouldn't stop asking her questions:

"Do you feel lonely with only one head?"

"Are you embarrassed because you aren't purple?"

"Why do you have all those hairs on your head?
Are they like antennas?"

Sal switched channels all night long, but by morning she was no closer to home.

On Channel Six Hundred and Ninety-Nine Thousand, Sal became a Chumpball in the *CHUMPBALL CHUMPIONSHIPS*. The worst part came when THE ROCKONS rushed on trying to catch her.

Finally, it was four o'clock, time for

back on Channel Two.

"Jack Dee Doobie!" Sal shouted. "I want to go HOME!"

"You tricked us, Sal," he said. "Your parts were no good. We're stuck on Earth. So you're stuck in Outer Space TV."

Suddenly, THE ROCKONS landed, shouting, "*RAU–AWK* Sal!"

"Help!" cried Sal. "They've been chasing me ever since I juggled them on *Gorbee Night Live*."

"Not chasing," said THE ROCKONS, "Following. Doobie's our friend! He needs parts! We got parts."

Jack Dee Doobie hugged all four ROCKONS. "Thanks, pals!"

"What about me?" asked Sal.

"You showed them the way here," said Jack Dee Doobie.

"So you win . . . A TRIP BACK HOME!"

The audience went wild.

"Press this blue button once
to go home," said Jack Dee Doobie.

"Press it twice for your Earth channels."

"What if I press it three times?"
asked Sal.

"Three times rewinds,"
said Jack Dee Doobie.

"You'll be back to when
you started."

When Sal got home, she could tell everyone had missed her.

They all shouted, "Where have you been since yesterday? We were worried sick. You're in big trouble!"

Sal knew what to do.
She pressed the blue button.

Once.

Twice.

Three times.

Everything was rewound—
back to when her family was
coming home from their walk.

"We had such an exciting
time!" her mother said.
"We think we saw a squirrel,
or maybe it was a bump
on a log."

"It was hard to tell in the
fog," said her father.

"Anything special on TV?"
asked her brother.

"I've had too much TV,"
said Sal. "I'm turning it off."

Her brother said, "Impossible!"
Her father said, "Unbelievable!"
Her mother asked, "Are you sick, dear?
Would you like a cup of warm milk?"

"No, thanks. I'll read Waldorf
his favorite book," said Sal.
"After supper, may I pick a
TV show we can all be on?"

"Yes," said her mother.
"But don't you mean a TV
show we can all watch?"

"Oh, no," said Sal. "I know
exactly what I mean."